Mary Murphy

I Love You

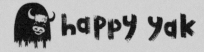 happy yak

To my good ol' pals, Louise, Fiona and Anne − M.M.

Mary Murphy has asserted her right to be identified as
the author and illustrator of this work.

First published in 2024 by Happy Yak, an imprint of The Quarto Group.
1 Triptych Place, London, SE1 9SH, United Kingdom.
T (0)20 7700 6700 F (0)20 7700 8066
www.quarto.com

A catalogue record for this book is available from the British Library.

ISBN: 978-0-7112-8902-4

Printed and bound in Slovenia by DZS-Grafik d.o.o.
9 8 7 6 5 4 3 2

Mary Murphy

I Love You

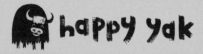 happy yak

I love you like
a bowl of juicy berries.

I love you like
a dandelion clock.

I love you like bamboo
with flyers flying through.

I love you like
sitting on our rock.

I love you like
a day at the seaside.

I love you like
pebbles in a pail.

I love you like a spade,
like lemonade.

I love you like a sandy trail.

I love you like
a crayon drawing dragons.

I love you like
a brush painting a star.

I love you like pink,
like jet-black ink.

I love you like
clean water in a jar.

I love you like
a boat on the river.

I love you like
a trick-track train.

I love you like a daisy,
like a ride when I feel lazy.

I love you like a zooming plane.

I love you like chicks,
like building bricks,

like summer showers,
like giving you flowers,

like a knock-knock joke,
like an invisible cloak,

like a little rock pool,
like a day off school…

What else?

I love you like mittens,
like tabby kittens,

like a careful snail,
like a gentle whale,

like a summer sky,
like a butterfly,

like a magic spell,
like a silver bell,

like a cockatoo,

like a kangaroo...

Phew!

I love you like
a picnic on a blanket.

I love you like
a yummy scrummy snack.

We're such a happy pair
and I'm a very lucky bear...

Because I know
you love me back.